The Quiltmaker's Gift

Story by
Jeff Brumbeau

Pictures by
Gail de Marcken

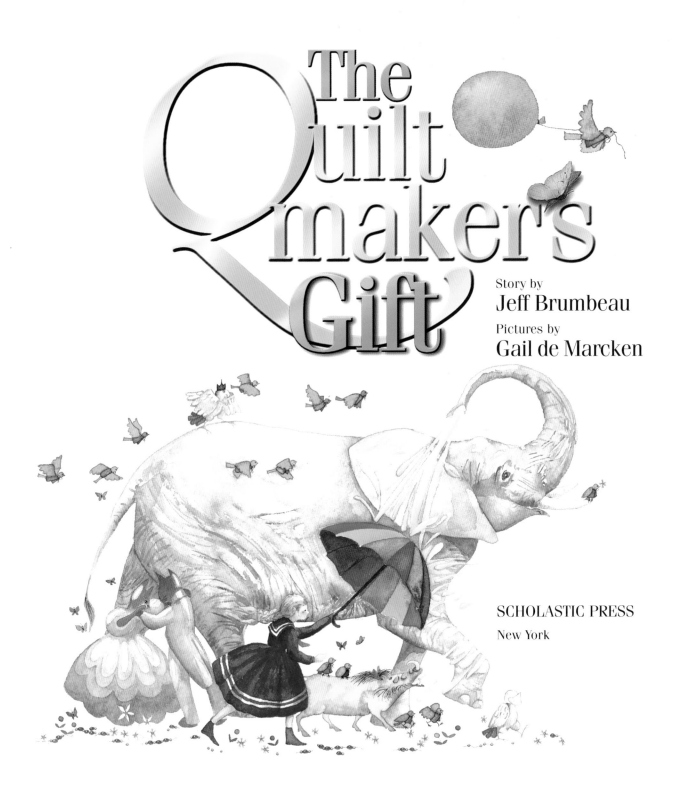

SCHOLASTIC PRESS

New York

The Quiltmaker's Gift

First Scholastic edition, March 2001

Printed in Hong Kong
by Palace Press International

10 9 8 7 6 5 4 3 2 1   01 02 03 04 05

Editorial Director: Nancy Loving Tubesing
Art Director: Joy Morgan Dey

Library of Congress Cataloging-in-Publication data

Brumbeau, Jeff
  The quiltmaker's gift / by Jeff Brumbeau : illustrations by
Gail de Marcken.
  48 p. 26 cm.
  SUMMARY: When a generous quiltmaker finally agrees to
make a quilt for a greedy king but only under certain
conditions, she causes him to undergo a change of heart.
  ISBN 0-439-30910-7
  [1. Quiltmakers Fiction. 2. Kings, queens, rulers, etc. Fiction.
3. Generosity Fiction.] I. de Marcken, Gail, ill. II. Title.
  PZ7.B82837 Qu 1999
  [E]–dc21

                    99-6547
                    CIP

For Marcia, who with the gift of herself has given me everything.

—Jeff

To B with love.

—Gail

There was once a quiltmaker who kept a house in the blue misty mountains up high. Even the oldest great, great grandfather could not recall a time when she was not up there, sewing away day after day.

Here and there and wherever the sun warmed the earth, it was said she made the prettiest quilts anyone had ever seen.

The blues seemed to come from the deepest part of the ocean, the whites from the northernmost snows, the greens and purples from the abundant wildflowers, the reds, oranges, and pinks from the most wonderful sunsets.

Some said there was magic in her fingers. Some whispered that her needles and cloth were gifts of the bewitched. And still others said the quilts really fell to earth from the shoulders of passing angels.

Many people climbed her mountain, pockets bursting with gold, hoping to buy one of the wonderful quilts. But the woman would not sell them.

"I give my quilts to those who are poor or homeless," she told all who knocked on her door. "They are not for the rich."

On the darkest and
coldest nights, the woman
would make her way down the
mountain to the town below. There she
would wander the cobblestone streets
until she came upon someone sleeping
outside in the chill. She would then take
a newly finished quilt from her bag, wrap
it around their shivering shoulders, tuck
them in tight, and tiptoe away.

Then the very next morning, with a
steaming cup of blackberry tea, she
would begin a new quilt.

Now at this time
there also lived a very
powerful and greedy king
who liked nothing better than
to receive presents.

The hundreds of thousands of beautiful gifts
he got for Christmas and his birthday were
never enough. So a law was passed that the
king would celebrate his birthday twice a year.

When that still wasn't enough, he ordered his
soldiers to search the kingdom for those few
people who had not yet given him a gift.

Over the years, the king had come to own
almost all of the prettiest things in the world.
Throughout the castle, from top to bottom,
in drawers and on shelves, in boxes and
trunks and closets and sacks, all of the
king's countless things were stashed.

Things that shimmered and glittered and glowed.
Things whimsical and practical.
Things mysterious and magical.
So many, many things that the king kept a list
of all the lists of things he owned.

And yet with all these marvelous treasures to enjoy, the king never smiled. He was not happy at all. "Somewhere there must be one beautiful thing that will finally make me happy," he was often heard to say. "And I will have it!"

One day a soldier rushed into the palace with news about a magical quiltmaker who lived in the mountains. The king stamped his foot. "And how is it that this person has never given me one of her quilts as a gift?" he demanded.

"She only makes them for the poor, Your Majesty," the soldier replied. "And she will not sell them for any amount of money."

"Well, we shall see about that!" the king roared. "Bring me a horse and a thousand soldiers." And they set off in search of the quiltmaker.

But when they arrived at her house, the quiltmaker merely laughed. "My quilts are for the poor and needy, and I can easily see that you are neither."

"I want one of those quilts!" the king demanded. "It might be the one thing that will finally make me happy."

The woman thought
for a moment.

"Make presents of everything
you own," she said, "and then
I'll make a quilt for you. With each gift that
you give, I'll sew in another piece. When at
last all your things are gone, your quilt will
be finished."

"Give away all my wonderful treasures?" cried
the king. "I don't give things away, I take them."
And with that he ordered his soldiers to seize
the beautiful star quilt from the quiltmaker.

But when they rushed upon her, she tossed
the quilt out the window, and a great gust
of wind carried it up, up and away.

The king was now very angry. He marched the woman down through town and up another mountain where he had his royal iron-makers shape a thick bracelet of iron. Then they chained her to a rock in the cave of a sleeping bear.

Once more the king asked her for a quilt, and once more she refused.

"Very well then," the king replied. "I'll leave you here. And when the bear awakens, I'm sure he will make a very fine breakfast of you."

Later, when the bear's eyes opened and he saw the woman in his cave, he stood on his mighty hind legs and gave a roar that rattled her bones. She looked up at him and sadly shook her head.

"It's no wonder you're so grouchy," the quiltmaker said. "You've nothing but rocks on which to rest your head at night. Bring me an armful of pine needles and with my shawl, I'll make you a great big pillow."

And that is what she did. No one had ever been so kind to the bear before. So he broke the iron bracelet and asked her to spend the night.

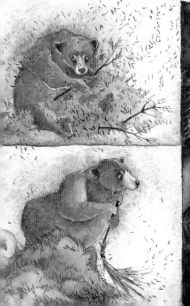

Now although the king was very good at being greedy, he was very bad at being mean. All that night he could not sleep for thinking about the poor woman in the cave.

"Oh my, oh my, what have I done?" he wailed.

So he woke up his soldiers and they all marched in their pajamas up to the cave to save her. But when they arrived, the king found the quiltmaker and the bear having a breakfast of berries and honey.

Now the king completely forgot about feeling sorry and became angry all over again. He ordered the royal island-makers to build an island barely big enough for the woman to stand on her tiptoes.

Once again the king asked her for a quilt, and once again she said no.

"Very well," the king replied. "Tonight when you're too tired to stand, and lie down to sleep, you'll drown." And the king left her alone on the tiny island.

Shortly after he left, the quiltmaker saw a sparrow flying across the great lake. A cold, fierce wind was blowing and it did not look like the poor bird would make it to shore. The quiltmaker called to him and he stopped to rest on her shoulder. The poor, tired sparrow was shivering, so the woman quickly made him a coat from scraps of her purple vest.

When he was warmed and the wind had stopped, the bird flew off. But he was very grateful to the quiltmaker for what she had done.

Soon the sky darkened as the air filled with a huge cloud of sparrows. Thousands of wings beating together, they swooped down, lifted the woman in their little beaks, and carried her safely to shore.

Again that night, the king could not sleep for thinking about the woman alone on the island.

"Oh my, oh my, what have I done?" he moaned.

So he woke up his sleepy soldiers again and they marched in their pajamas down to the lake to set the woman free. But when they arrived, she was sitting on a tree limb sewing tiny purple coats for all the sparrows.

"I give up!" the king shouted. "What must I do for you to give me a quilt?"

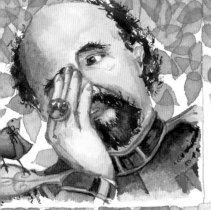

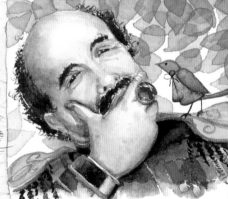

"As I said," the woman answered, "give away all of the things you own and I'll sew a quilt for you. And with each gift that you give, I'll add another piece to your quilt."

"I can't do that!" cried the king. "I love all my wonderful, beautiful things."

"But if they don't make you happy," the woman replied, "what good are they?"

"That's true," the king sighed. And he thought about what she had said for a long, long time. So long that weeks went by.

"Oh, all right," he finally muttered, "if I must give away my treasures, then I must!"

The king went to his
castle and searched from
top to bottom for something
he could bear to give away.

Frowning, he finally came out
with a single marble. But the boy who received it
smiled so brightly in return, the king went back for
more things.

Eventually, he brought out a pile of velvet coats
and went about the town, giving them to people
dressed only in rags. All were so pleased that they
marched up and down the street in a grand parade.

Still, the king did not smile.

Next the king fetched a hundred
waltzing blue Siamese cats and the dozen
fish that were clear as glass.

Then the king ordered
his merry-go-round with the
real horses to be brought out.
Children cried with delight and
cartwheeled around him.

And just the smallest of smiles began to show
on the king's face.

The king looked about him and saw the dancing and merrymaking and all the happiness his gifts had brought. A child took hold of his hand and pulled him into the dance. Now the king really smiled and even laughed out loud.

"How can this be?" he cried. "How can I feel so happy about giving my things away? Bring everything out! Bring it all out at once!"

Meanwhile, the quiltmaker kept her word and started making a special quilt for the king. With each gift that he gave, she added another piece to his quilt.

So the king kept
on giving and giving.

When at last there was no
one left in town who had not
received something, the king
decided to go out into the world and
find others who might be in need of his gifts.

But before he left, the king promised the
quiltmaker he would send a sparrow back to her
each and every time he gave something away.

Morning, noon, and night, the wagons rolled
out of town, each piled high with the king's
wonderful things. And for years and years,
messenger sparrows flew to the quiltmaker's
windowsill as the king slowly emptied his wagons,
trading his treasures for smiles around the world.

On and on the quiltmaker worked, and piece by piece the king's quilt grew more and more beautiful.

Finally, one day a weary sparrow flew into her window and perched on her needle.

She knew then and there that it was the last messenger, so she put a final stitch in the quilt and started down the mountain in search of the king.

After a long search, she finally found him. The king's royal clothes were now in tatters and his toes poked out of his boots. Yet his eyes glittered with joy and his laugh was wonderful and thunderous.

The quiltmaker unfolded the king's quilt from her bag. It was so beautiful that hummingbirds and butterflies fluttered about. Standing on tiptoe, she tenderly wrapped it around him.

"What's this?" cried the king.

"As I promised you long ago," the woman said, "when the day came that you, yourself, were poor, only then would I give you a quilt." The king's great sunny laugh made green apples fall and flowers turn his way.

"But I am not poor," he said. "I may look poor, but in truth my heart is full to bursting, filled with memories of all the happiness I've given and received. I'm the richest man I know."

"Nevertheless," the quiltmaker said, "I made this quilt just for you."

"Thank you," replied the
king. "I'll take it, but only if
you'll accept a gift from me.
There is one last treasure I have left
to give away. All these years I've saved it just for
you." And from his rickety, rundown wagon
the king brought out his throne.

"It's really quite comfortable," the king said.
"And just the thing for long days of sewing."

From that day on the king often came to the
quiltmaker's house in the clouds.

By day the quiltmaker sewed the beautiful
quilts she would not sell, and at night the king
took them down to the town. There he
searched out the poor and downhearted,
never happier than when he was giving
something away.

Visit the quiltmaker and the king online at
www.QuiltmakersGift.com
where you will find:

 Puzzles and games from
The Quiltmaker's Gift.

 Stories of generosity from
around the globe.

 Quilt block lore and quilting
activities for all ages.

 Contests and prizes.

 Conversations with the
author and artist.

Jeff Brumbeau, Gail de Marcken, and
Scholastic Inc. have joined in dedicating
a portion of the revenue from
The Quiltmaker's Gift to projects that implement
the spirit of generosity portrayed by
the quiltmaker and the king.

Wild Goose Chase

Trail of Friendship

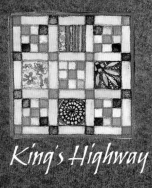
King's Highway

Friendship Star

Snail's Trail

Rosebud

Crazy Quilt

True Lovers' Knot

Next Door Neighbor

Trip Around the World